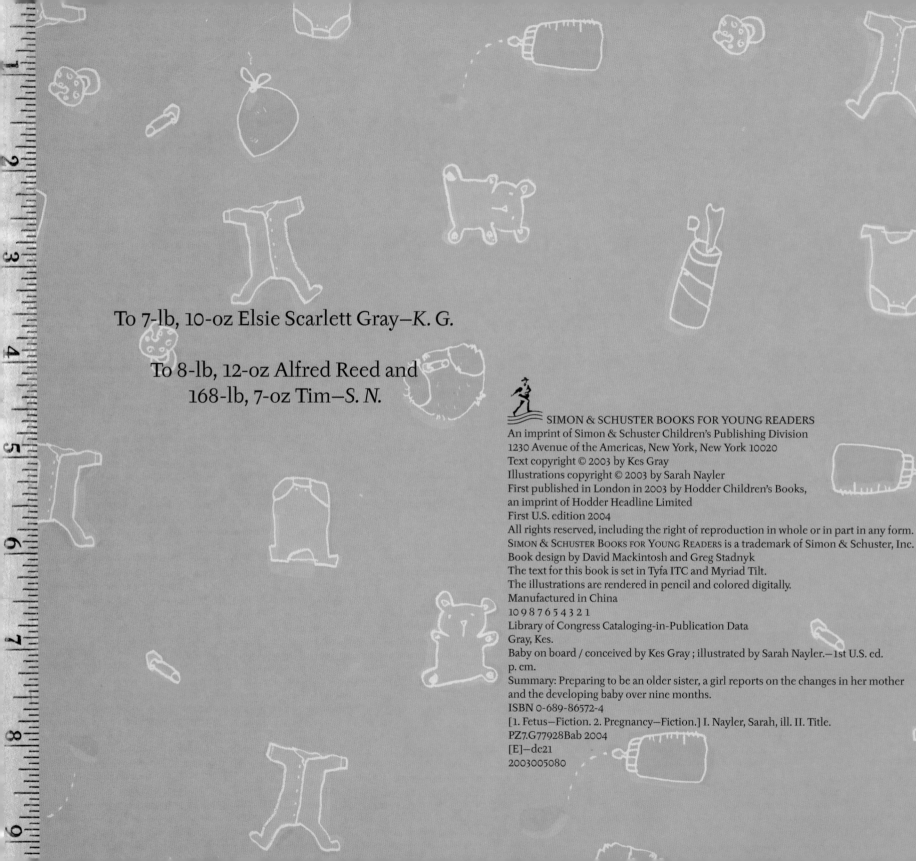

To 7-lb, 10-oz Elsie Scarlett Gray—*K. G.*

To 8-lb, 12-oz Alfred Reed and
168-lb, 7-oz Tim—*S. N.*

SIMON & SCHUSTER BOOKS FOR YOUNG READERS
An imprint of Simon & Schuster Children's Publishing Division
1230 Avenue of the Americas, New York, New York 10020
Text copyright © 2003 by Kes Gray
Illustrations copyright © 2003 by Sarah Nayler
First published in London in 2003 by Hodder Children's Books,
an imprint of Hodder Headline Limited
First U.S. edition 2004
SIMON & SCHUSTER BOOKS FOR YOUNG READERS is a trademark of Simon & Schuster, Inc.
Book design by David Mackintosh and Greg Stadnyk
The text for this book is set in Tyfa ITC and Myriad Tilt.
The illustrations are rendered in pencil and colored digitally.
Manufactured in China
10 9 8 7 6 5 4 3 2 1
Library of Congress Cataloging-in-Publication Data
Gray, Kes.
Baby on board / conceived by Kes Gray ; illustrated by Sarah Nayler.—1st U.S. ed.
p. cm.
Summary: Preparing to be an older sister, a girl reports on the changes in her mother
and the developing baby over nine months.
ISBN 0-689-86572-4
[1. Fetus—Fiction. 2. Pregnancy—Fiction.] I. Nayler, Sarah, ill. II. Title.
PZ7.G77928Bab 2004
[E]—dc21
2003005080

Baby on Board

Conceived by Kes Gray

Illustrated by Sarah Nayler

Simon & Schuster Books for Young Readers

New York London Toronto Sydney Singapore

There's a baby growing
in Mom's tummy.

NEWS
Flash

I'll keep you informed!

One month:
He's a teeny-
weeny blob,
less than a
quarter inch
long.

Mom's really smiley and her cheeks are all rosy. Dad says that's because she's blooming. He wants to call the baby Doug. Mom says no blooming way!

Two months:
He's half a
piece of
chewing gum
long.

He's still a blob, but his arms and legs
are beginning to grow. Dad wants
to call him Bob.

Three months:
  He's as big as
    Mom's thumb.
  He's got eyes,
    but he
      can't
        open
          them!

I guess it's too dark inside Mom's tummy to see anything anyway. Mom feels sick every morning. Dad says maybe we should call him John.

Four months: His teeny, tiny fingers have teensy-weensy fingernails.

Mom's felt him wriggle.
Dad says we should call him Elvis.
Mom keeps eating pickled onions.

Five months:
He's about the size of an action figure
but nowhere near as muscular.

When I put my hand on Mom's tummy, I can feel the baby kick! Dad thinks he's going to be a soccer player and that we should call him Pelé. Mom says Dad should think again.

P.S. She's buying bigger bras.

Six months: He still hasn't opened his eyes yet, but he's as long as a ruler and as heavy as Biffo's dinner.

Dad thinks we should call him Hulk because he's bound to be a wrestler. Mom keeps wanting to wee.

Dad thinks he's going to be a really tall basketball player and that we should call him Michael.

Boo!

P.P.S. Mom's buying bigger panties, too.

Eight months: He's as long as my arm.
His brains are growing really fast,
he's opened his eyes, and guess what?

He's turned upside down!

Dad reckons he could have gymnast potential and that we should call him Sergei. Mom gets cranky a lot at the moment. She needs a pillow under her bump to help her sleep.

Nine months: He's still upside down. He looks like a real person, and he's ready for launch.

Dad has packed a bag to take to the hospital. Inside it's got Mom's medical notes, some diapers, boob cream, ladies' things, a nightie, a hairbrush, a scrunchy, three pairs of panties, a toothbrush, slippers, Dad's sports magazine, and his Game Boy.

Dad says Mom should practice her breathing.
Mom says Dad should practice sleeping on the sofa.

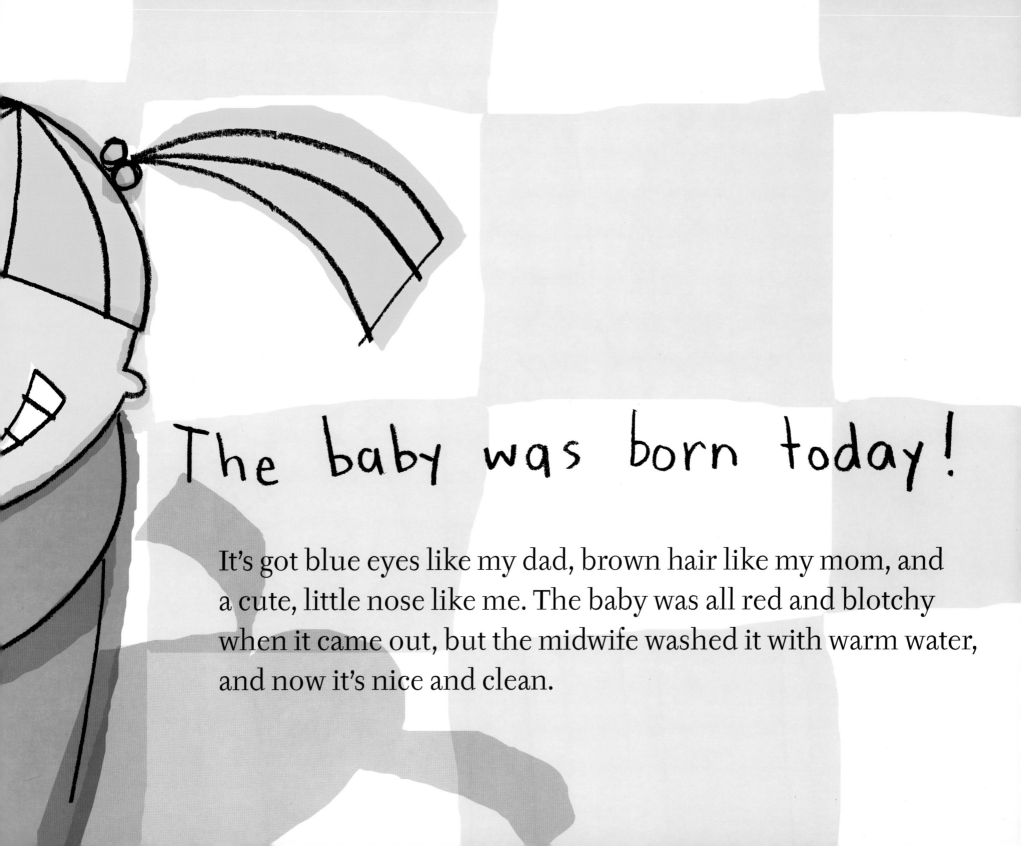

The baby was born today!

It's got blue eyes like my dad, brown hair like my mom, and a cute, little nose like me. The baby was all red and blotchy when it came out, but the midwife washed it with warm water, and now it's nice and clean.

I'm really excited.
Dad's really proud and
Mom's sick of pickled
onions.

I think a better name
might be Susan.

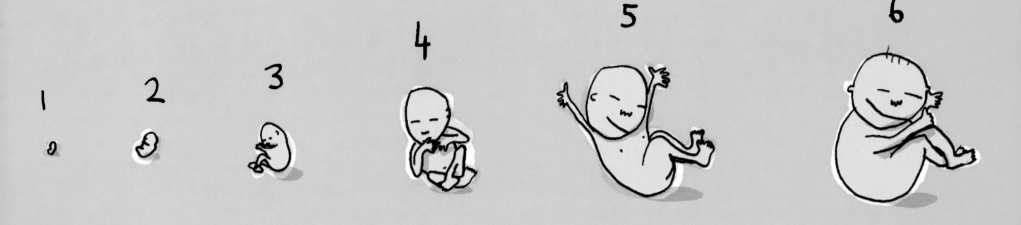